For Chelsea and Felicity
—E.B.

For Amelia, Zak, Emma, Isaac, and Owen
—A.C.

THIS IS A NEW YORK REVIEW BOOK
PUBLISHED BY THE NEW YORK REVIEW OF BOOKS
435 Hudson Street, New York, NY 10014
www.nyrb.com

Text copyright © 1973 by Ellen Blance and Ann Cook
Illustrations copyright © 2020 by Quentin Blake
All rights reserved.

ISBN 978-1-68137-428-4

Cover design: Leone Design, Tony Leone and Cara Ciardelli
Cover art: Quentin Blake

Manufactured in South Korea.
Printed on acid-free paper.

10 9 8 7 6 5 4 3 2 1

Meet Monster

The First Big Monster Book

Ellen Blance and
Ann Cook
wrote this story.
Quentin Blake drew the pictures.

The New York Review Children's Collection
New York

A NOTE TO PARENTS

The stories in *Meet Monster* were originally created for beginning readers. They are unusual because we developed the text from conversations we had with children, paying attention to their vocabulary and cadence. Quentin Blake's illustrations also provide abundant visual clues to support children in becoming independent readers. The stories remain popular for emerging readers, and, of course, can also be enjoyed as read-aloud stories to share and discuss with your child. We'd very much like to hear about your child's response to *Meet Monster*.

—Ann & Ellen

Contents

Monster Comes to the City   1

Monster Looks for a House   25

Monster Cleans His House   43

Monster Looks for a Friend   69

Monster Meets Lady Monster   95

Monster and the Magic Umbrella   121

Monster Comes to the City

Once upon a time
there was a city.

A monster comes
to this city to live.

Monster is not ugly
like other monsters.
He's kind of tall and
his head is skinny.

Monster goes
around the city
to see the river
and the houses
and everything.

He goes up the lamp post
to see the houses
and the cars.

He goes
to the railroad station
to see the trains
and everything
and what the people
look like.

Then he goes to the park
to see the kids.

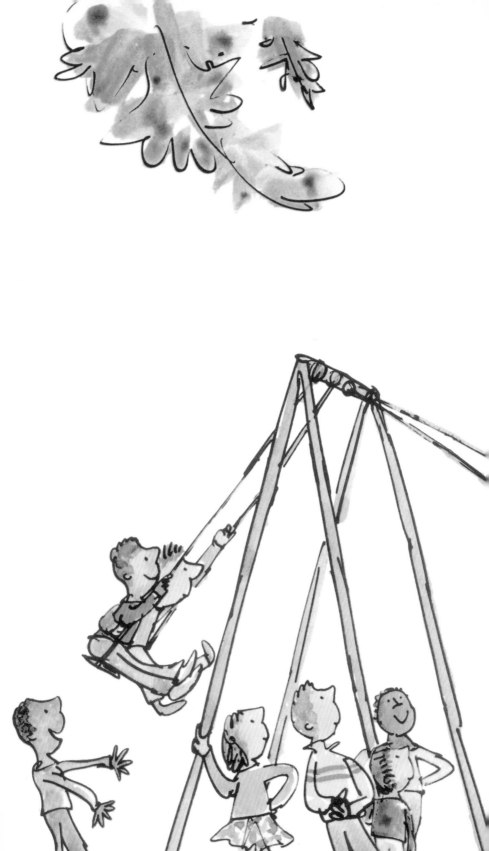

He goes to the park
to play with the kids
swinging on the swings.

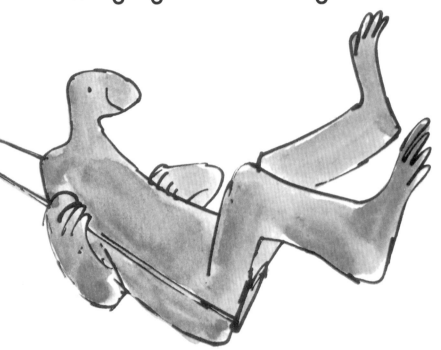

He looks at all the stores and clothes and stuff.

He gets all packed up.

Monster thinks
the city is fine
so he thinks
he will live here.

Monster Looks for a House

Once upon a time there was
a city.
A monster comes to live in
this city.

He looks at the map.
He wants to find a place to live.

He is going on the bus to see
where he wants to live.

He thinks he likes this street.
He might be able to live here.
He looks at all the houses.

This house is dark all over.
Not many things happen in
this house.
He can't live here.

He likes the bell on the top but
this house is too big for him.
He can't live here.

This house is a mess.
Monster can't live here.

Monster finds a pretty house
that is too little for him.
It is too little.
He could hardly fit in here.
Monster can't live here.

He might be able to live in
this house.
It's tall and thin.
The windows are just right for
him—and the door.

He goes into the house.
He says it's OK for him.
It's very comfortable.
It's very, very fine.
So he will live in it.

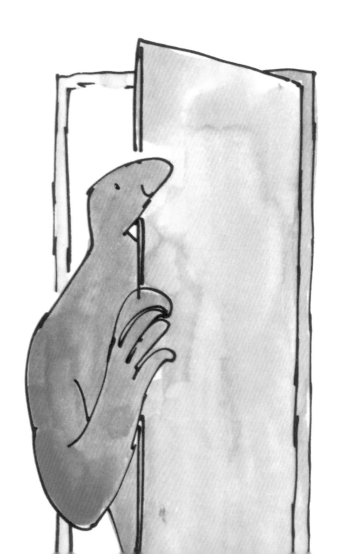

Monster Cleans His House

Monster lives in a tall
thin house in the city.
He loves the house.
It's very, very fine.

He's got a bedroom,
a bathroom, a closet,
a living room,
and a kitchen.

It's kind of nice
for a monster.
It's kind of comfortable.

Monster loves the house.

He's reading a book
about monsters because
he's a monster himself
so he should read
a monster book.

He thinks
he will clean the house
so that if children want
to visit him it will look
really fine.

He cleans the bedroom
so that if people come
to his home to sleep
he won't have to clean
the house when
they are sleeping.

He cleans the kitchen
so that when people come
and want to cook
for Monster they can.
The kitchen won't be all
messed up.

He cleans the bathtub
so that
when people come in
to take a bath
they won't get dirty
and when they turn
the water on,
the water won't get dirty.

He cleans the closet
so that people can put
their clothes inside
and the clothes
won't get dirty.

Monster thinks
he's done enough cleaning.

He's kind of tired
and sits down.
The house looks really fine.

Monster Looks for a Friend

Monster loves his house.
He likes to eat his
breakfast in bed.

He is thinking about
what he should do today.
Monster thinks
he will go out
to play ball.

Monster plays ball
for a long time.

He loves to play ball
but it is not fun
by himself.

Monster is very sad
because nobody is around
to play with him.

He sits on the ball
and he is very, very sad.

He goes out of the house
to find somebody
to play with.
He takes his umbrella
and goes out to look
for a friend.

He goes in all the streets
to see if there are children
to play with but
there aren't any.
I don't know why.

He looks in the houses
but he doesn't find
anybody to play with.
It isn't raining
so I don't know why
he takes the umbrella.

He looks in the park
but he can't find anybody
to play with.

Monster comes back
to his house.

He is sad.
He is really,
really sad
because he can't find
anybody to play with.

Next to the door
of his house
is this little boy.
"Maybe he's lost,"
says Monster.

The little boy says that
he likes the house.
He says to Monster,
"Can I live in it?"

So Monster says,
"Sure, sure,
you can live with me.
You're my best friend."
And they shake hands.

Monster Meets Lady Monster

Monster said he wanted
to clean up the house today.
The little boy wanted
to go play outside.

The little boy wanted
to play ball instead of
cleaning up the house.
He thinks it's not fun
cleaning up the house.

Monster gave the little boy
an apron.
Monster said, "Here,
put on your apron
so you can help me.
You can wash the windows."
The little boy looked mad.
I think he was sad.

The little boy looked
out of the window.
He saw another monster,
a lady monster.
He thought there wasn't
such a thing as
another monster.

She was playing
jump rope with two hands
and her feet going
up and down.
She was looking pretty.

The little boy went upstairs
to tell Monster.
But Monster couldn't hear him.

So the little boy yelled:
"There's a lady monster
outside!"

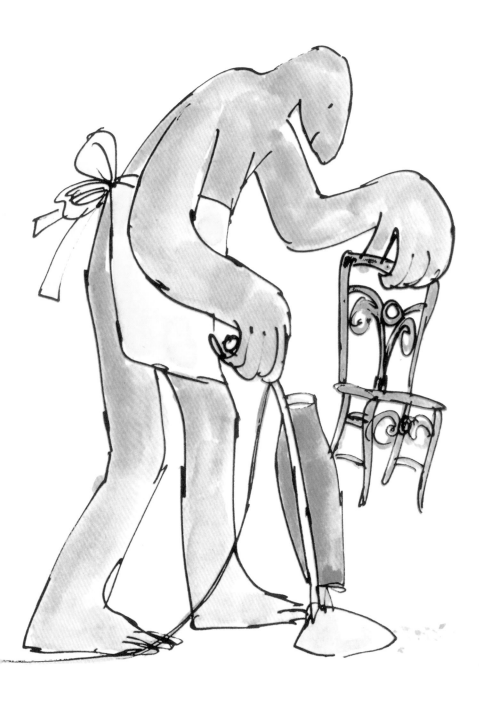

He yelled in his ear:

"There's a lady monster outside!

There's a lady monster outside!

There's a lady monster outside!"

Monster was happy.
He was so, so happy.

He went into the bathroom
and brushed his teeth
and brushed his hair
and put on his beautiful tie.

Then he said,
"Can I play with you?"
The lady monster said,
"I'll be glad to have you
play with me."

Then the man monster
fell in love
with the lady monster.
And they jumped rope
together and had
a very good time.

Monster and the Magic Umbrella

One day Monster
and the little boy
got out of bed.
The day was so hot.
The sun was shining.
So Monster said,
"Come on, let's wash up
and get dressed
so we can go outside
and play."

So that's what they did.
It was such a hot day.
So Monster got his best hat
and his umbrella
to keep the sun off
his face.

Then everyone played ball.
The sun was shining
on them.
They smelled sweaty.

Then all the boys
and all the girls went off.
Their mothers called them
for dinner.
Monster and the little boy
felt so hot.
The little boy said,
"Oh, Monster,
I feel so hot."

So Monster opened
the umbrella
to keep the sun off
their faces.
"Now it'll be much cooler,"
Monster said.
So that's what Monster did.

He just opened his umbrella.
Then the umbrella grew
bigger . . .

. . . and bigger.

Then Monster turned it
around.
Boy, wasn't it giant-sized!
Super big!
So the little boy
and Monster just looked.
Then the little boy said,
"Oh, Monster,
I wish we had
a swimming pool
to swim in.
I'm so hot."

Suddenly
big drops of water
fell in the umbrella.
Then the little boy said,
"Oh boy!
Doesn't that look
like a swimming pool!
Let's take off our socks
and shoes and jump in
and take a swim."
Monster said,
"Yeah, why not."

The water was all cool.
It felt so good.

The boys and girls
came back out.
All the boys
and all the girls
took their shoes off.
They jumped in
and just splashed the water
up and down.
Up and down.

Then, "Home for bed,
home for bed,"
everybody said.
Everybody said,
"Let's do that tomorrow.
That's really fun."

So the umbrella
got smaller and smaller
and tinier and tinier.

Then the umbrella wasn't
a magic umbrella anymore.
Then Monster
and the little boy
went to their house
to go to bed.
The little boy said,
"Maybe we can do that
tomorrow, Monster."
So Monster said,
"Yeah, maybe we can."

ELLEN BLANCE grew up in the northeast of England. She moved to London in 1964 and attended the University of London in order to study alternative methods of developing language and reading skills for children. In 1970 she was invited to work with New York City teachers. She taught classes at the New School and at City College. Ellen joined the staff at Bank Street College where she worked on the desegregation of the Stamford, Connecticut, schools. She also worked with teachers in Mamaroneck and Rye Brook, New York. Now retired, Ellen spends some time in New York City and Connecticut schools reading the *Monster* books and talking about writing to enthusiastic young writers.

ANN COOK works with children and teachers in New York City public schools. She directs a consortium of schools that have replaced standardized testing with performance assessment, allowing students to demonstrate their knowledge and skills. She is the author of three series of books for beginning readers and of numerous articles for adults about child-centered education and teacher collaboration. A collector of children's books, she particularly enjoys reading to her five grandchildren.

QUENTIN BLAKE is one of the most celebrated children's book illustrators working today, having illustrated more than three hundred books by such authors as Russell Hoban, Joan Aiken, and Roald Dahl. A prolific writer of books for children himself, he was appointed the first Children's Laureate of England in 1999.